Kiss in the Rain

The story of three valentine's days of three different individuals…linked together by one bond… but what went wrong..? Read to find out…….surely love is myth..!

Khushi Gupta

ISBN 1234567890123345
© Khushi Gupta 2021
Published in India 2021 by Pencil

A brand of
One Point Six Technologies Pvt. Ltd.
123, Building J2, Shram Seva Premises,
Wadala Truck Terminal, Wadala (E)
Mumbai 400037, Maharashtra, INDIA
E connect@thepencilapp.com
W www.thepencilapp.com

Author biography

Khushi is a crazy die-hard romaticism fan, who wrote this novella years ago as a teenager, most of the writing must be screaming that immaturity quite loudly! This is just a fun attempt to celebrate the innocence of those years.

CONTENTS

Introduction

The story of three valentine's days of three different individuals…linked together by one bond… but what went wrong..? Read to find out……surely love is myth..! Before we begin with the story, the writer would like to share here the significance of the title- "KISS IN THE RAIN". It is quite obvious that the title suggests that the story is a romance but beyond that it has a deeper meaning to it. 'Kiss' is known to be the ultimate touch of affection , the ultimate indication of the love between two individuals in any relation…beyond which nothing seems to be meaningful. Similarly, 'Death' is also the ultimate touch of heaven, the ultimate call from God…beyond which everything seems to be false. Thus a kiss is metaphorical of death. On the contrary, 'Rain' has always been believed to be the most beautiful gift of God, for which we can never thank him enough. It takes away all our worries and miseries in a fraction of second and leaves us delighted but always unfulfilled. Likewise , 'Love' has also been believed to be his most thankful creation. Love lifts us off our sorrows and provides us a pleasurable world but seldom leaves us satisfied. Therefore, rain is metaphorical of love. Thus the complete title – 'KISS IN THE RAIN', actually means 'LOVE BEYOND DEATH'.

The Second Valentine's

10:00 pm

Tuesday

14th February 2009

"Now calm down and tell me what happened..?"-Adi asked Sana over a coffee in a local coffee bar in Pitampura. She heaved a big sigh. Her eyes still a bit wet. She looked around and saw the place happily swarmed by smiling couples . Of course…its valentines eve…she thought to herself. Suddenly last year's valentine's day buzzed past her eyes. "it was a lovely evening…"—she said half lost. "huh--?" "14th February 2008 ….. my last valentine's day with Sameer. I was wearing a black dress that he'd gifted me. He said black suited me best." Adi noticed that right now also she was wearing a black shirt with trousers. Its been one year since Sameer's demise now but Sana could never recover from the trauma. Though Adi had been with her all through but emotionally they could never connect. Adi didn't had the minutest idea of the turmoil in Sana's mind. She spoke after pauses-- " I couldn't imagine then life would take such a turn in just an year…." She tossed a black diary on the table. " this is Sameer's diary…Anvesha{Ashi} gave it to me." "diary… Sameer never told me that he wrote diary.."-Adi was taken aback. "neither was I aware….. till now." Adi picked up the diary and sifted through it.

Miss Hunterwali

Wednesday

2 nd July 2oo7

Dear diary

Today was the first day of college. I was hell nervous but the day went on smoothly. I made quite a few nice friends. You know Adi and me had a blast. No one could rag us. We were rocking man..! The best thing that has happened is my best friend Adi with me since school days and we are now in same college too..! I met a girl today…quite decent by looks . it was her first day too and we are in same course. She walked in with a guy a typical nobody..! and it was evident by her expressions that she too was struck with the idiot. A group of guys walked towards them {some seniors probably} encentering a frail looking nerdy. One of them spoke-"your name and courses …quick." "Sana…B.Com first year"—the girl spoke. "Harsh….B.Com first year"-- her friend spoke. "are you brother and sister"—the group asked half mockingly. "no..we are just friends."-Harsh replied. " great then …kiss each other." "are you guys crazy…he's my best friend's boyfriend..!"-Sana screamed on them.. "ya right guys don't be crazy .. she's my girlfriend's best friend"—Harsh agreed. "hey hey hey…we don't mind that..kiss each other right now in front of us. We are your seniors obey us right away." "you look at this guy", one them said pointing to the nerdy-" he's the nephew of this college's principal, we'll get you suspended for a week" " I don't mind that either..get me suspended then… either ways this college sucks like hell..!"—Sana echoed. " whoa girl..what tantrums of the princess…see you then outside the college…!"-they laughed. "why… are you guys gonna accompany me there?"-she reverberated. "no miss hunterwali….we're gonna bid you bye-bye.." "to hell with you"-she said angrily. "hey…I don't wanna get suspended.. I can kiss anybody else.."-Harsh exclaimed " bloody wimp.."-Sana walked away fuming. As she was about to leave a guy remarked—" hey girl, have any issues kissing me?" "no … but get him to kiss you. Either ways he's too desperate"- she said pointing to Harsh. The girl surely has great deal of guts… she refused to get ragged by seniors..! That moment I made up my mind that I wanna talk to her. I'll try tomorrow.

Thursday
3 rd July 2007
Dear diary
It was a lovely day. I talked to that girl Sana… remember I told you 'bout…..ya right miss hunterwali… She's cool yaar… I'll tell you how we gotta know each other. I entered the classroom and she was sitting all alone. I asked her if I could join her and she agreed. Then in middle of class I asked.. "hey miss hunterwali….err…." She gave me some stern cold looks-"Sana…Sana Ahuja" " 'm so sorry actually yesterday when you were busy handling those bunch of idiot seniors, I was there too so all I could remember was this stupid name"-I defended myself. I actually realized by her looks that the name suited her the most. " my name's Sameer Raghvan " "hi.."-she replied

half convinced. I dared not utter a word for next fifteen minutes or so. Her dangerous looks made me shrug. Then I gathered all my guts and spoke-" so are you genuinely interested in this subject or there's anything wrong with me?". She looked at me and then smiled-" no nothing like that. Its just that we don't know each other so I thought that you must be studying." "oh..no..no..no..lady. don't get deceived by my intelligent attitude and smart looks. Its been quite a very long time since I've dropped the idea of gaining knowledge in this temple of education….in simple words.. like all others I study a day before exams" "so are you usually so over confident or something special today?"- she asked laughing. "naa…..just trying build an impression" "I thought so.."-she replied. "coffee..?"-I asked her after the class. "sorry am sort of in a hurry..sometime later maybe..?"-she replied. And there goes my first chance I thought –"ya sure…see ya soon then". But am not gonna lose my heart like this. The girl has got a certain charm that killed me like hell. The pangs that I get when I talk to her or the joy that I get when I make her smile that's really unfathomable.

Night Night

"That night Sameer messaged me", Sana continued "he has not mentioned that here. Probably 'coz it was too late at night. That was the first time we talked out of college."

Hey..what you doing-Sameer

Nothing much as of now-Sana

Wanna talk? - Sameer

I don't mind - Sana

"hi"-Sameer called up. " hi..what you doing 12.00 midnight..aren't you feeling sleepy"-I asked him. "no…seems as if you too have lost your sleep..what happened?"- he asked me. " nothing special.. just lost in thoughts."-I replied. "Great….thinking is my favorite pastime too….. helps kill loads of worries…."-he supported. "Naa… nothing big a trouble…. Just thinking 'bout Harsh." "oh…that Mr. kiss-me-all….?" "wha-at?…….ya right….funny name"-I smiled. "what's his issue….he's not even your guy I guess…" "true…he's actually my best friend Mahi's boyfriend….I just told her about that ragging incident……she was upset like hell…." "oh…that's bad….I think you should be talking to her right now…."-he said. "no.. she's busy with her studies right now…she can't afford to lose on to that just because of that loser Harsh….you see she's in medical college…" "okay" "so are you regretting that you imposed their breakup..?"-Sameer asked me. "no…I didn't impose their breakup….they were already on the verge of it. Harsh has not been that caring of late as he used to be earlier…..since the time the school got over, he was already eyeing other girls…and Mahi was pretty much aware about it . this was just another tale to add to it."- I explained. "oh…so there's nothing exactly you could do to help them. Why are you worried then?"- Sameer asked me. " I'm not worried but I was just wondering one thing. It was Harsh who insisted on their relationship. He was so caring during school time. But now…,he has changed completely. It seems he's not the same person now as he used to be." "hey angel…look, some people are good at pretending while some others are good at calling a spade a spade…its up to an individual of how you want yourself to be portrayed. Might be that he was genuinely interested in your friend at that time and later he discovered that they weren't compatible."-he explained. "but this is not the way to change ways… does he expect her to discover that on her own?"- I demanded. "maybe… that's what I am trying to explain…maybe he's just good at pretending and that's why he finds it difficult to confess that he's not interested anymore…he wants HER to say 'its over' " " that's actually funny.."-I commented. "funny or not but its human nature…"-he agreed. "anyways…you were telling about Mahi….is she pretty? She must be single now , right?"-he asked. "ya right…she's pretty, good looking, sexy and unavailable…"-I laughed out. "unavailable ….? But why…?"-he asked disappointed. "b'coz she's a nice girl and she's my friend …you better stay away…"-I commanded. "even I am your friend and a nice guy who's single…just see if you could help…?"-he asked. "Sameer….! Get lost now….stay away from my friend and now lemme sleep…"-I argued. "hey…

this is not fair…! I helped you overcome your thoughts and now you refuse to help me…I tell you what…you are just jealous if I talk to your friend..”- he talked insanely like a 5-year old. "Whatever Mr. Psychologist…this is 'human nature'." —I laughed off. "I just loved teasing him like that. He looked so cute when he demanded things like a 5-year old child. That was the first time I discovered the true SAMEER. His ideas of relationships were awesome. I could feel the virginity of his thoughts flowing through me." -Sana spoke to Adi.

I heart you

Adi's cell phone rings. He excuses himself to attend it. "hi Ashi, …. Ya she's fine and we are together right now…….ya just tell her mom first…..we'll come when she feels like……don't worry yaar……ya right…..okay fine…..hey-….hey….hey…. I can manage Ashi….just relax……okay yaar m sort of busy…..talk to you later…..bye..!!" "strange yaar, Ashi and me have been together since one and a half year now but she never told me about Sameer's diary."-Adi was puzzled. "it was because of me… Anvesha gave the diary to me within a week of Sameer's death and it has been with me since then. I asked her not to tell about it to anybody."- Sana explainedAnvesha was Sameer's sister who was one year younger to him. Despite the fact that their friend circle almost coincided, they were miles apart from each other. And that was quite evident from their frequent cat-dog fights and arguments. But all their friends knew that they were ready to die for each other in troubles like any other siblings or best friends, because they were seldom separated from each other. Adi and Anvesha were in a relationship since around 18 months and Sameer knew about it. He was in fact happy about it.

Wednesday13th august 2007Dear diaryIt was our fresher's party today. After dropping Sana home after the party, all of us headed to the club for our private party. Though I was not interested at all and in fact quite upset because Sana had to leave early, I was dragged there by Adi. Soon everybody was drunk and they were all dancing merrily. I very forcefully avoided hard drinks. Just when I asked Adi to move back home and dumped him in the car, he began blabbering senselessly, I heard him confessing that he loved Ashi very much. I was half shocked and laughing at the same time, both because the dog never told me anything before. I drived down to my place and called up Ashi and asked her to open the door. She angrily got out to open the door after mincing a few words . she too was taken aback on seeing Adi in drunk condition. I said to her-"you won't believe but this idiot actually likes you…!!!" She had a mix of emotions happiness, amazement, astonishment, anger all at the same time. Obviously never ever in her dreams would she have imagined her first crush proposing her in drunk state through her brother….!!! She shouted on both of us- "you two are imposturous…!", and went away fuming. So tonight I am sheltering Adi, Ashi's anger and their yet to prosper relationship that started with a fight… Poor guy would kill me once he knows after waking up that what I did for a favour to him…!! now I should better call up Sana in order to avoid another fight..!

"I remember laughing over the entire incident when he told me over phone later…!"- Sana smiled a bit. "ya right…..and I remember that one week that I wasted away to cool down Ashi's anger. I cursed that moment when I was drunk ….and then one week hence of pleadings, Ashi forgave me only on the condition that I propose her officially on a romantic dinner…!!"- Adi recalled. Sana was all smiles to this. Adi noticed a smile on Sana's face after a very long time. For a second he too was lost in her smile that was very comforting. "Sana you look great when you smile…."- Adi complemented. And with this a tear trickled through her already smudged eyes. "what happened…?"- Adi asked. "nothing…."-Sana replied forcing a smile.

Friday22nd August 2008Dear diaryI was sitting by myself in the evening today. Sana was a bit busy and since Adi and Ashi's relationship started, I hardly get to talk to Adi except in college so it was pointless to call him, I thought. Just then Ashi entered my room and sat besides me in the balcony, quietly. I asked her why wasn't she talking to Adi right now, she replied- "that idiot had to go to a family function…". "wow, now I get to know about my best friend through my sister…!". She punched me lightly on my arm and asked how was everything going on… "life is strange…it makes you dream of a future that is far from your reach…."-I replied. "don't you have more simpler words to say that you are missing Sana in your life…..?"- she asked me. "what….? I wasn't talking about Sana at all…hell I was just---- " I was interrupted in between. "oh c'mon bro…we might not be sharing each other's life stories but we are quite connected through souls…. I know you more than you yourself…!!"-she argued. "you read my diary again..?"-I asked. "….actually yes…last night after you dozed off…!"- she confessed. " damn ….. I hate you for this…."- I shouted. " okay…okay..am sorry….but the point is that you should tell everything to Sana before anybody else proposes her and you will be reduced to a mere agony aunt….!!"- she changed the topic. "ya right and what if she refuses….? I can't put our friendship on stake…."- I said. "look…you are some-what human looking and nice by attitude to others so I see no point in her refusing you….just give it a shot , bro…"-she walked away before I could explain any more excuses. Damn…. I guess I'll have to confess my feelings to Sana….. lets see what happens.

Love is a myth

"Sameer called me up later at night. We were talking in general when he raised the topic abruptly about love."-Sana recalled. " so Sana, have you ever been in a serious relationship..?"-he asked me. "no..never…"-I replied. "any particular reasons for that?"- he asked again. "I don't know Sameer… you are my close friend so I can confess you things that I have never talked about with anybody… I actually find it funny how people enter in a relationship through an institution called 'love'".- I replied. "why…I mean what's funny…?"- he inquired. "I …I …I don't know…ok leave it…anyways you won't understand.."-I tried to duck the question. But he was insistent-" c'mon Sana…you think I am so insensitive?" "nothing like that yaar…ok I'll try to explain….its actually funny how we grow up playing 'husband and wife' and then gradually as we grow up, we are wired to believe that actually we have our soulmates waiting for us in some distant land who would give us all the pleasures of the world and all their love……we get married …face the realities of life…and later realize that it was nothing but a cruel joke of god….because actually nothing called 'love' exist…its all a myth that's been prevailing since ages….!!"- I burst out. "oh my god…you don't believe in love..?" "see…I told you ….people don't get my point of view…."-I replied. "but there has to be a reason to it …?"- Sameer asked. "

everything has a time Sameer…you don't know anything about me yet and I don't think its right for me to disclose anything right now..''- I tried to explain. " angel …. I don't know what's on your mind right now ….but all I can say is that love is meaningless if you don't believe it but it is the most beautiful creation of god if you trust it…and as far as love being a myth is concerned, everything fades when it is bound to…relationships die, people die, love die…but we must enjoy it till it lasts….''- Sameer explained. "ok leave it but why were you asking such things in first place?''- I asked. "just like that…nothing special..''- he replied sheepishly.

Chini is my life

Monday

25th august 2008

Dear diary

It was an awesome day today. I have been away from Sana the whole weekend and today in the morning she started shouting at me in the college in morning. "Where the hell have you been the whole weekend…. Mr. Sameer Raghvan…..?"-Sana screamed at me in front of Adi and few other friends of mine. "What's wrong with you Sana…."-I asked her looking around consciously. Then I took her to canteen and ordered two cups of coffee and asked her to calm down. "Relax Sana… what happened..?"- I asked. " what happened…? I have been calling you since past two days continuously but no reply…even Adi didn't know where were you….do you realize how worried I have been…?"- Sana wasn't in a good mood yet. "but I wasn't in Delhi Sana actually Friday night grandpa called up saying that chini wasn't well and she was constantly murmuring my name…so I left early Saturday morning for my grandpa's home in Chandigarh and I forgot to carry my cell phone in a hurry so I couldn't tell you about the plan..''- I defended myself. "who's chini? ''- she asked suspiciously. " chini is my life Sana…. She's my first love….she stays with my grandparents in Chandigarh and we've been playing together since childhood….we've actually grown together…she's the sexiest female alive on this planet…!!"- I exaggerated. "but you never told me about her.."- she asked. "everything has a time Sana …."- I retorted back. "ya right ….sorry I forgot that you have your personal life too…so how's she doing now?"- she asked with a hint of sarcasm. "she is now fine…she was suffering from mild fever… she's gone pale and weak…gosh I couldn't see her…it was heart-breaking …. But I still miss her…" "so you should be with your chini right now….why did you come back….?"- Sana asked me. "oh…I too wish I could be there but dad called me back….he simply doesn't understand my love….!!"- I replied back. "so…how serious are you with her..?"- she asked me. "meaning..?"- I asked back. "meaning….do you both plan to get married..?"- Sana asked me. " what…???? Why would I marry a cat…..??"- I coughed a bit. "chini is your cat…..????"- Sana was taken aback. "of course she is my cat…..you thought she's my girlfriend….oh Sana……how could you even imagine something like that…?"-I teased her. "but you were describing like…..oh forget it…I am sorry for that…..!"- she was embarrassed and turned red. She smiled a bit with relief , looked up and murmured something to herself. I loved her even more at that time. She looks so cute with those burning eyes and jealous looks. Her anger vanished in a minute. "that's really ohkay…!"- I exclaimed. "so..you rushed all the way to Chandigarh for a cat…???"- she asked me again teasingly. "yeah…so what….? I love her a lot….!"- I defended myself. She grinned at me . I asked-"what…?". "aawh nothing…",she replied suppressing her laughter

Swollen Eyes

"you were jealous of his cat…?"- Adi inquired from Sana. "he called her the sexiest female alive on this planet…can you imagine that…how on earth could I guess that chini was actually his cat...??"- Sana defended herself again. Just then a waiter came to both of them and said-" excuse me sir, sorry ma'am, we are very sorry to disturb you on this lovely evening but we wanted to inform you that its 12 midnight , one hour past our usuall closing time…" Both of them looked around and noticed that earlier crowded café was now completely empty except for a few workers staring at them and smiling among themselves. They both got up and left the place embarrassingly apologizing. They walked out of that place on streets…the roads which were usually choked with traffic in the sunshine gleamed now in solitude bathing in the yellow streetlight.

The silence though killing for Adi but it was now a part of Sana's life. "Sana….I know it is difficult for you to forget the past but you need to overcome it…if Sameer was alive he would never have let you stay so depressed."- Adi broke the silence. " Adi…there are some decisions that you take for your life while some others that the life takes for you…it was Sameer's decision to enter my life, god's decision to snatch him away from me….and now its time for me to enforce some of my decisions for my own future. People teach you a lot in their lives but Sameer taught me a lot even in his absence….friends like you helped me sail through the difficult times while some others left me only upon the slightest smell of a trouble….”- Sana replied.

She continued, “ I still remember the days just after his demise when I was completely shattered…my school days’ friend, Mahi used to visit me to change my mood. She used to coax me to move out and try and forget him. Often she got frustrated on seeing my miserable condition and then one day both of us lost it.” “Sana why the hell don’t you realize that Sameer is history…he’s not coming back again.”- Mahi shouted at Sana.

“Mahi its easy for you to advice sitting at the other end…Sameer is my life….he promised me that he would never leave me alone… how could he forget that promise…?? How could he forget me..?”- Sana was in tears again. “life has not ended for you, Sana. You are still young, beautiful , educated, and independent…if you look around people are waiting there with thousand times the love that Sameer offered..!!”- Mahi argued. “ Mahi are you out of your minds…you want me to betray Sameer..?? I would kill myself but never would I even think of somebody else….”- Sana retorted back. “fine then…no arguments to that…its better that I leave…but remember Sana…you are destroying yourself in madness of one years’ stupidity…don’t turn blind to the love that’s in offering from your family and friends…you are hurting them in the way…just look at the pain in your mother’s eyes when she sees you in this condition…”-Mahi replied back, getting up to leave. “the day you yourself are in love , that day you will realize my position. The thing that you call stupidity is actually 'love'…if you can't understand me today, maybe you don't desearve to stand by me for the rest of my life…!!"- Sana warned her. Mahi left the place shrugging her head in disbelief. "….that day I realized that even lifelong friends can leave you in trouble if they are not true…its better to let go a relationship than to hold a false one…"- Sana said with a hushed tone. "if you don't mind can we sit on that bench and continue…I don't wish to go home today…"-Sana asked Adi. "ya sure Sana…"- he replied.

They both moved to a bench on the pavement, then Sana rest her head on Adi's shoulder. "I am tired Adi…tired of life…tired of slogging alone…tired of keeping things to myself.…that is why I decided to talk to you, because after Sameer, you are my closest friend."- Sana said in a low tone.

Please friend tonight
Don't ask how don't ask why
Just gimme your shoulder
And lemme cry
Just gimme your arms
And lemme die
I am full from within
Just wanna burst now
Hold me with faith
Hold me tight
From dusk to dawn
Just wanna scream
Just wanna shout
Don't plead sanity

Don't swear love
Just gimme your arms
And lemme die
For Christ sake
Please kiss my pain
My world's burning
Hell broke down
Don't ask how don't ask why
Just gimme your arms and lemme die
I know you care
But please don't speak tonight
Till my eyes dry
Just lemme cry
Please friend tonight
Don't ask how don't ask why
Just gimme your shoulder
And lemme cry
Just gimme your arms
And lemme die….

"Sana…you left home without telling anybody..we were actually worried that you might attempt to end your life."- Adi said to Sana. "Ha... Adi...if suicide was ever on my mind, I would have attempted it just after Sameer was gone…but his memories never allowed me something as horrendous as suicide…he once said to me that suicide is one of the biggest crime because if you cannot give new life to this world, you don't even deserve to take away your own life.. as it is a gift of God and by suicide you are actually disgracing God …no problem can be solved by ending our own lives …it is only a way of shifting them to your loved ones…his words never ever allowed me to even think of suicide…"-Sana explained. "After that day we talked a lot on various topics of interest. We got to know each other better, likes, dislikes, etcetera… we got so close to each other that we couldn't live without talking to each other even for a single day. We met each others' parents and that only grew us closer. And then on 2nd September, exactly two months after we first met each other, Sameer proposed me."-Sana told Adi.

The Proposal

Tuesday

2 nd September 2008

Dear diary

Today I proposed Sana. Though it was supposed to be the most beautiful day of my life but…... Today both of us bunked college together for the first time. I took her to Rajeev Chowk and after roaming for two hours there, we settled on a quiet bench. Suddenly it started raining heavily. I got up and started looking for shelter. And then just as I was looking hurriedly around, I noticed Sana….. her eyes playfully enjoying the shower, her cheeks red probably in admiration of the nature's bounty(or of the fear of her first college bunk…I don't know…?), the way those little droplets of rain were dancing on her pink lips, and her tresses blown out of her face by the wind…..I was lost diary,…I was lost in Sana….then she looked at me and started laughing …..She asked me, "hey Mr. know-it-all, you're looking for shelter as if you're made up of salt, afraid of getting wet ?". I snapped out of my dreams and smirked. "No angel, but what are we gonna explain to our parents back home…got wet in class…?" I replied. "Gosh, Mr. Topper, I know you've loads of grey matter with you but some things need use of heart and not brains….!" She replied. I laughed at this and came back to join her where we were sitting before. "so is this your first date?" I asked

Sana. "date…?? You call this a date…what's the occasion?" she counter questioned me. "I mean we're out together for the first time…I guess this is called a DATE" I replied. She coughed a bit and then suppressing her laughter "Sameer, I am sorry I didn't knew you were so desperate (then actually breaking out laughing) that you'd call a bunk with your friend a date…!" ."hey …stop calling me that I am NOT desperate" I defended myself . "oh really, ohkhay then tell me how many girlfriends you've had?" she teased me a bit more. "well I've had two girlfriends and three crushes till yet. So I am not desperate." "wov…impressive…and do these supposedly two girlfriends of yours know that they were your girlfriend at that time?" she asked me. "what do you mean?" I couldn't get her. " I mean are you sure that those were actually RELATIONSHIPS and not like this DATE of ours?" she was at it again, how she loved pulling my leg all the time….!! " funny Sana, very funny…!" I replied. She broke out laughing at this. I could have had all the insults to my name if only she promised to keep laughing like this all the time, I thought to myself. She was today in her that mood when anything and everything could make her laugh for hours at a stretch and I just loved her like that. " hey icecream…I want ice-cream…" Sana started shouting like a kid. "ice cream now….in this rain…?". "yes I want ice cream right now…" she demanded. I rushed to mc Donald's and got two chocolate cones. Then I raised the topic again "Sana do you like me?". "even if I don't Sameer, I've no option left. I've already promised you a life long friendship" she replied without much efforts obviously not serious again. "Sana I am serious" I asked the same question again. "obviously yaar otherwise why the hell would I've been sitting here with you?" she replied. Then as she was about to get up to move back I said those words " Sana Ahuja I love you….". she looked at me in astonishment and I stared back with affection. And that was our last gaze at each other for today. She said nothing at that moment but weirdly stepped back from me , "Sana where are—" , " SHUT UP…SHUT UP….!!" She shouted at an interval and then ran away alone. I don't know what has happened to her all of the sudden. I thought she loved me too.ok diary Adi has come home and now I stop here.

The heartbreak

"I had never seen him more disturbed before that night. He was losing his sanity at that time", Adi continued "I took him outside to change his mood after he told me what had happened between you two. I offered if I could talk to you and explain everything since you were not responding to his phone calls but he refused my assistance." Adi took a deep breath and then closed his eyes and then continued as if not wanting to remember that night again.

10:00 pm

Tuesday

2 nd September 2008

"Adi, you know how I feel for her yaar. I just told her my feelings is love a crime? Why doesn't she understand this thing. She isn't even responding to my calls. She's never ever reacted this way" Sameer told Adi. "maybe I or Ashi could help make her understand this thing" Adi suggested. "no yaar, this is between me and her I don't want to make this appear as an issue" Sameer declined the suggestion. "you know what Adi…maybe this is my fault…I shouldn't have said those words …maybe I should've just let my feelings die down…at least…at least I could've saved our friendship…now I am …I am…I have lost a friend Adi…I have lost a friend…I am doomed…I am…"

Sameer break down crying. "Sameer nothing is lost yaar just try to explain things to her. Try to talk to her and even if you two are not together as mates you could still be friends for life….calm down" Adi tried to console him. Sameer nodded " I am not sure but I'll still try". "yes champ that's the spirit man…c'mon now lets go to Naraina and lets eat some paranthas" Adi tried to cheer him up. "no yaar not today some other time" Sameer avoided. " chal na yaar , my treat" Adi coaxed further.

" how can I forget that day…it was so beautiful . my first college bunk with Sameer and then when everything was going perfect, he proposed me…and then I lost my cool" Sana continued, " the next day we met in college and we couldn't avoid each other. Despite being so cross with him I just couldn't live without Sameer because before everything else, he was my best friend. After the college was over we moved together to talk."

 4:30 pm
Wednesday
3 rd September 2008
"Sana I am so sorry I didn't mean to hurt you yaar but …please Sana lets just forget whatever happened yesterday and lets just talk like before…I …I don't wanna loose a friend in you" Sameer tried to explain Sana. "Sameer you know what, yesterday was my most beautiful day, until you said those words…I've told you Sameer…that I don't believe in love…why can't we leave our relationship to just friendship…" Sana was now calm as ocean, something in her heart never allowed her to part ways with Sameer. "that's what I want to know about you Sana. You said we are friends, right? So for the sake of our friendship I want

to know why my first true love could never be completed…its important for me to know Sana" Sameer asked her with the same innocence with which he had proposed her. Both of them partly exhausted with the day's work and partly by the friction between their thoughts decided to sit in central park for some time. It was about to dusk by that time. The diffused sunlight had already formed a picturesque pattern on the canvas of sky holding a different meaning for both of them . Sameer knew that this rosey sky was holding a rather devastating thunderstorm within it and maybe he was ready for it too. But Sana didn't had the minutest idea that this thunderstorm would actually bring a beautiful rainbow with it in her life. "ok if its so important for you to know the reason, Sameer this feeling 'love' has left no pains to snatch away all my spirits in life, it has always weeded my happiness, it has always eclipsed my joys and now I am rather afraid of it" Sana explained. "please be clear Sana, I can't understand you" Sameer said. " Sameer, my parents had a love marriage… against the wishes of my both set of grandparents. They were in love, so they married against the wishes of their parents", Sana stumbled with words for a few seconds and then she continued " and you know what…just because of this, my grandparents separated themselves from my parents… can you imagine Sameer, they didn't bothered to even see the face of their first grandchild till… till I was four years old…one relationship broke the rest of them…where was this 'love' gone at that time Sameer…?". Sana choked and gulped a little water. "when I was ten years old, eleven years after my parents' marriage, they both separated….'love' left them…my dad fell for another women…sounds like another melodramatic cheapster from a stupid movie…,isn't it? But this is my life Sameer, I have no time for love" Sana remarked as she got up from her place, her eyes closed and arms encircled to hug herself. "you know why I reacted that way yesterday, since the day I met you, I started liking you…so much so that I couldn't live without talking to you even for one day…I got a friend in you Sameer, a best friend…but this word 'love' got on my nerves…I thought that everything will be shattered now…I got afraid Sameer…afraid to loose you…" Sana finally break down without looking at Sameer. Sameer got up and moved closer to Sana, he pulled her hand slightly and jerked her towards him "Sana , what are you afraid of? Do you stop walking if you fall once? Or do you stop living just because you know that you have to die one day? Things have not been easy and they would never be, but you know what, let yourself free for a moment…enjoy the present Sana" "its easy for you to say that dammit just because its not happening to you…" Sana shouted wildly. "I've seen my mom crying…crying for love…and you know what…it kills inside to see her break down helplessly" she declared. Pause.

"You can certainly build that wall to save your heart from bruises but you can never stop me from loving you Sana" Sameer concluded the conversation. Nobody spoke anything henceforth.

Promises

"hey, what are you staring at ?" Sana asked Adi as she stopped recalling. " no just thinking how much pain, anguish and bitterness could a face so lovely hide" Adi remarked. "what happened after that? How did you melt?" Adi asked. "love never knocks before it enters…it just seeps in never to leave again, same happened with me. Sameer was there for me every time I needed him. You know what Adi, anybody can understand your word but Sameer could even understand my silence. It was beautiful Adi…our understanding…to laugh uncontrollably over silly things, sharing silence together, crying for minutes together, sitting and glaring at the stars, or enjoying ice cream together in rain .His fighting with the whole world over a drop of my tear and then unintentionally making me cry. Sameer was right, I could never stop him from loving me. He gradually overtook my stiffness towards love" Sana replied

4:30 a.m.

Wednesday

15th February 2008

The fog was about to clear up and the darkness still embraced the sky. it was yet another winter morning and the sun still slumberous in the clouds. "I think we should leave now before the sunrise" Sana said as she got up to leave. "I couldn't understand one thing Sana, why did you say that Sameer is back when you called up last night ?" Adi asked. Sana pulled out a brown covered file from her handbag and passed it on to Adi. "what's this…?" Adi inquired. "my reports" Sana said calmly, "I've been diagnosed with pancreatic cancer….just one month before I'll be gone with Sameer , to his world,…"

"SHUT UP SANA…..this is all bullshit….you are not going anywhere….just stop this nonsense right now" Adi was frustrated. He flew down her hospital reports. "this is faux Sana…we'll get you treated to a good chemotherapist….you are not leaving us…these bloody government hospital doctors don't know anything--" Adi shot back. "Dr. kalra is my family doctor since I was three years old, Adi. And she is a reputed medical practitioner since past thirty years. We trust her diagnoses very well. And chemotherapy doesn't help in malignant form" Sana was still free from any sort of emotional surpass. Adi was thrown down on his knees due to such a sudden shock.

Every time I close my eyes
Friend I see you there
I fear to shed my tears
'coz I don't wanna loose you
I don't know what happened n why
But I just need you
I wait for you here
Hope you miss me too
I am mad I know
But friend you promised to hold
Me with care
Friend I am weak

Please walk slow
I'm bleeding here love
Shit I don't wanna loose you
I don't care if I die
But I can't live without you
Just wish your picture to be colorful
Even if its painted with my tears
Friend I'm weak
Please walk slow
Just wanted to remind you
That I still need you….!!!

"he has fulfilled his promise Adi….Sameer fulfilled his promise" Sana was at it again. Adi looked up in disbelief, "what promise?" "the promise that he made before he left me", Sana recalled

The First Valentine's

7:30 p.m.

Thursday

14th February 2007

"Sameer , where are we going? And can I remove this cloth from my eyes? I want to see where are we heading exactly" Sana asked Sameer. "no angel, just wait till we reach there. You'll get to know everything. trust me on that" Sameer smiled. "and yes angel, whether you believe or not, but this is officially a date…." Sameer continued. "positive" Sana laughed it off remembering their first outing together. Sameer drove all the way to gurgaon and parked in front of a local mall. Then they carefully walked together towards a dine-in place with Sana still blindfolded. Then Sana was allowed to open her eyes. she opened her eyes and was left gaping. They were standing on the seventh floor of the mall in an open space of the dine-in place and in front of them was a beautifully done up place full of florescent lights and decorations. The floral arrangement perfected the picture perfect settings with scented atmosphere. The background was complemented by remixes and melodies. Both of them moved towards an empty table to make themselves comfortable. "sorry I couldn't get this complete place booked just for the two of us as they show in movies…it costed a fortune…!!" Sameer said apologetically. "shut up Sameer it was totally unnecessary…I mean we could have done with a cheaper dinner…why all this formality?" Sana punched him lightly. "never mind yaar I'm already out of this month's pocket money so without any formalities all my expenses are yours this month after this date…!!" Sameer laughed off. "Sameer….!!!" Sana giggled. Just as both of them were waiting for their order to turn up, Sana looked around with a bored expression, "gosh…one more minute with this super boring pianist and I'll be reminded of my bed back home….could it get more torturous than this?" "hey Sameer why don't you sing a song for me and everybody else , I guess everybody around here is equally bored as I am" Sana chirped. "you kidding..? if I start singing a song around here, either I'll be bashed up badly or everybody will leave disgusted" Sameer ducked the request. "you can't even get bashed up for your baby, sweetheart?" Sana blinked her lashes with her most innocent of expressions. Sameer took a deep breathe " am already killed by your smile so who cares for these junk of a crowd…ok I'm ready to entertain my angel. And even if these people leave it'd be good for us…will get the time alone…!" Sameer winked at Sana. Sameer walked up to the dais and whispered something in the ears of the lead singer to which the singer gave him a guitar and left the dais.

"This is for my angel SANA to whom I've dedicated my whole life. Artist 'Enrique Iglesias', song name 'addicted' " Sameer announced.

Have I told you how good…
it feels to be me…
when I'm in you…
I can only stay clean…
when you are around…

so let me be…
if I close my eyes forever…
can I be myself …
can I see again…
maybe I'm addicted…
I'm out of control…
but you're the drug that keeps me from dying…
maybe I'm a liar…
but all I really know…..
is that you're the only reason I'm trying….

Sameer sang so well that he left his audience mesmerized. He made the evening memorable for everybody including Sana. the two left the place after dinner. The rain started as they moved on. On the way home, Sameer turned the car to an isolated lane. "I think you're heading wrong" Sana warned. "I never chose the wrong way, I'm heading absolutely right , angel" Sameer shot back. "overconfidence is dangerous" Sana smiled. "but confidence is required to achieve success" Sameer said as he halted the car midway. "and why do you think you'll succeed in the way you've chosen Mr. Sameer Raghvan?" Sana said with a confident mysterious smile. " because you're with me SANA" Sameer answered back with eyes straight in hers. " Sana I'm not afraid to face the world if you promise to stand by me always" Sameer was still gazing at her eyes.

"I'm afraid Sameer"

"of what?"

"of love"

"do you trust me?"

"more than God"

"so promise me.."

"what?"

"promise me that 50 years hence when all your hair will turn white but still you'll look drop dead gorgeous, you'll be gazing at the blue sky and remembering the old times…promise me that at that time you'll tell your grandchildren that their grandfather was a brilliant singer and…"

"and…?"

"and…" Sameer continued in a hushed up tone " an awesome kisser…" Sameer bent over Sana and they kissed each other. "promise" Sana replied afterwards, "but you need to make me a promise too…" "ya sure what's that ?" Sameer asked. "that you'll never ever leave me alone come what may" Sana asked. "oh ya sure never.." Sameer replied casually and bent over to kiss again. "I'm serious Sameer" Sana stopped him. Sameer took a deep breathe and answered " ya sure angel I promise I'll never ever leave you alone come what may" Sana smiled at him "now lets move back" "so early ?" Sameer formed a frown with a drooping lip. "Sameer its already quarter to ten, mom must be worried" Sana tried to explain. "ok then as you wish…." Sameer started the car to move back

Dusking life

"and then after he left me home, just ten minutes past that, I got a call from his home that he's had an accident on his way back home with an over speeding truck, a case of drunken driving" Sana said recalling every minute detail of that fateful night. "he promised me that night Adi, that he'll never ever leave me alone come what may…and see …he's fulfilling his promise…he's taking me away from here too…he's taking me along--" "stop it Sana…please stop for god's sake…stop…" Adi said with his silent sobs turned to full fledged wails.

Sana was advised complete bed rest for rest of her time. Pancreatic cancer was making her physically misbalanced. She'd grown pale and weak in a matter of time. At times she couldn't eat or sleep properly just because of her pain in upper abdomen that radiated to her back. The cancer had invited its friends along with it, jaundice and diabetes mellitus. She was reduced to a blob living on drugs and needles. Her mother who'd already lost hopes from life was often seen shouting in dreams, taking off her frustration from life. Sana's depression was too evidently inevitable. At times, she used to sit ideally not talking to anybody just staring at the wall ahead, and at times as jovial as if it were her last day. She used to cry on petty issues and fight more often with her mom. But all this while, Adi was with her every moment, every second. He was the one who could make her laugh even while crying and cheer her up in worst of situations. Adi used to console her mother too on occasions as and when necessary. Her days started with Adi and ended with thinking about Adi. Both of them used to spent hours at a stretch together in gardens, staring the dew covered grass and the clear sky at night. They used to talk endlessly in rains so that Sana won't be reminded of her past and of Sameer again. Adi cut himself off from rest of his social circle just to be with Sana. Often he used to fight with his girlfriend Ashi as they were spending less time together and whatever little time they got together was gone talking just about Sana.

And then one day…………..

"and then Sana started crying…..", Adi was talking to Ashi over phone. "Adi….I …", Ashi interrupted. " Ashi ….Sana has become soo sensitive these days that…", Adi overlooked her interruption. " SANA…SANA…SANA…gosh I've got fed up now…will you please shut up now..?" Ashi shouted. "what's your problem Ashi…why you being so insensitive?" Adi spoke out of obliviousness. "I've become insensitive Adi..? you're the one who's treating Sana like a goddess…" Ashi spoke bitterly. "you know why I'm supporting her that much still you're not understanding me Ashi…?" Adi asked her. " Adi I've lost my individuality in your life in the mean time" ,Ashi tried to explain with her raised up tone. "nothing like that yaar I love you a lot Sana--", Adi fumbled as he inadvertly spoke out the wrong name. " ASHI….ANVESHA RAGHVAN…" , Ashi spoke as she paused to hold back her breathe to avoid crying.

"Ashi…look I'm sorry--", Ashi cut the line as Adi tried to explain. Adi tried to reach her back but things never turned out to be as they were before. And it seemed as if Adi was least bothered to make it work even. He was too engrossed in keeping up with Sana. This is how Sana ended a relationship without even intending to. As her last days approached, distances between Sana and Adi grew shorter. Sana refused to meet any other relative or friend in her last days except her mother and Adi. Adi used to do all her daily chores. He used to sit with her, tie her braid, eat with her, take her around for walks, bear her screams, give her a shoulder to cry, and in between if possible, make her smile. Sana shouted on him, hit him, kicked him, punched him, but at last he was the only one who could make her laugh. At times Sana used to remain silent for three to four days at a stretch speaking nothing but just shouting and at time she used to sob silently just staring at Adi.

4:30 p.m.
20th February 2009
Friday
Adi was reading Sana a book. Suddenly Sana held his hand tightly and spoke, "Adi, why does it rains?" Adi silently closed the book and kept it away. He took her hand in his and while staring deeply into her eyes he spoke, " Sana , God is one and he cannot be present every time with everyone and so he created rain to wipe out our worries", he paused as he noticed the dark spots under her eyes and was reminded of several sleepless nights that she spent just crying….hours after hours….days after days…months after months….he could feel her pain in those eyes that were now tired of even beaming. He stretched out his hand towards the window on which little moist settled due

to rain, he gently wiped out its portion to feel the dew on his fingers and spoke afterwards , "Sana, God has sent rain ma to wipe our tears….so that we don't miss his presence." " Adi, hug me…" Sana demanded. Adi hugged him tightly for more than a minute and as he released her, he realized she was still than ever. He tried shaking her and even called out her name several times but she was gone. He rested her head back to the pillow and kissed her on her lips.

The Third Valentine's

8:30 p.m.14th February 2010SundayAdi sat in the same coffee house as he and Sana were, exactly one year ago.

Dearest Sana,Sorry, I didn't go to college, I wasn't feeling well. I guess I've got a cold. But don't worry, I've taken medicine and I'll be fine soon. I've tried waking you up several times but you don't respond to me Sana. Please don't do this to me. Look, you are testing my patience now. How long will you keep sleeping. I'm getting bored alone now and you have to get up to speak to me. Okay I promise I'll take you out the next time it rains but please don't be angry now. Now I think we should finish this coffee soon and move back before these waiters ask us to get lost…!! I love you a lot Sana.Yours Adi.

Adi finished writing in a thick brown diary and as he capped his pen back and closed his diary, he looked ahead and noticed the café crowded with young couples. He was reminded of last years' valentines' day. He smiled within himself and gulped down the last sip of his coffee.